The Legend of Minnesota

By Kathy-jo Wargin

Illustrated by David Geister

To Ed and Jake. You are my heart.

Kathy-jo

For Pat, Eva, and Allie, the strong women in my life.
Your love sustains me.

David

Sleeping Bear Press™
310 North Main Street, Suite 300
Chelsea, MI 48118
www.sleepingbearpress.com

THOMSON
GALE™

© 2006 Thomson Gale, a part of the Thomson Corporation.

Thomson, Star Logo and Sleeping Bear Press are trademarks
and Gale is a registered trademark used herein under license.

Printed and bound in Canada.

First Edition

10 9 8 7 6 5 4 3 2 1

Library of Congress Cataloging-in-Publication Data

Wargin, Kathy-jo.
The legend of Minnesota / written by Kathy-jo Wargin ;
illustrated by David Geister.
p. cm.
Summary: "This is the story of an enduring friendship between an Ojibwe girl and
a Dakotah boy, and how their kindness towards one another brings healing to a tribe,
and gives the beautiful land of Minnesota its name"—Provided by publisher.
ISBN 1-58536-262-X
1. Ojibwa Indians—Folklore. 2. Ojibwa mythology—Minnesota—Juvenile literature.
3. Minnesota—Folklore. I. Geister, David. II. Title.
E99.C6W314 2006   398.209776—dc22

About The Legend of Minnesota

The definition for the word "Minnesota" is known to most as the Dakotah word for "sky-tinted waters." In 1879 while addressing the Minnesota Historical Society on the history of Lake Superior, General James H. Baker noted a comparable Ojibwe name for the wooded northern portion of the state. The word *Mah-nu-sa-tia*, also known as *Maanizaadi* to the Ojibwe, was used to address all land west of Lake Superior. It means "balm of Gilead," or "balsam poplar."

When author Kathy-jo Wargin discovered an age-old version of a legend titled *Mahnusatia*, published in 1893 as part of a collection of Minnesota legends, she began to research other versions of the tale. In her version for children titled *The Legend of Minnesota*, we learn the story behind the land of the balsam poplar and the enduring friendship between an Ojibwe girl and a Dakotah boy who want nothing more than peace between their people. Because of their kindness toward each other, generations that followed came to call the beautiful land "Mahnusatia," which according to the legend, in other accents spoken became known to all as "Minnesota."

Long ago in the land of lakes, where pine-wrapped bays made half-moon shapes among ancient rocky vales, was one lake known to all. As dark and deep as the moonless night, it became a sea of yellow and orange with every setting sun, and was so named for its colors, "vermilion." Beyond this lake was a mountain, grim and gray and sacred, where the riches of time not yet discovered, the ore of iron, lay quietly stowed and waiting.

To its people, the Ojibwe, the land was an abundant place. There were blueberries to pick and fish to spear, grains of wild rice to harvest and maple sap to boil into hard cakes of sugar. It was a time of plenty, but it was not a time of peace. The Ojibwe were at war with the Dakotah, and the two tribes had not seen calm in many years.

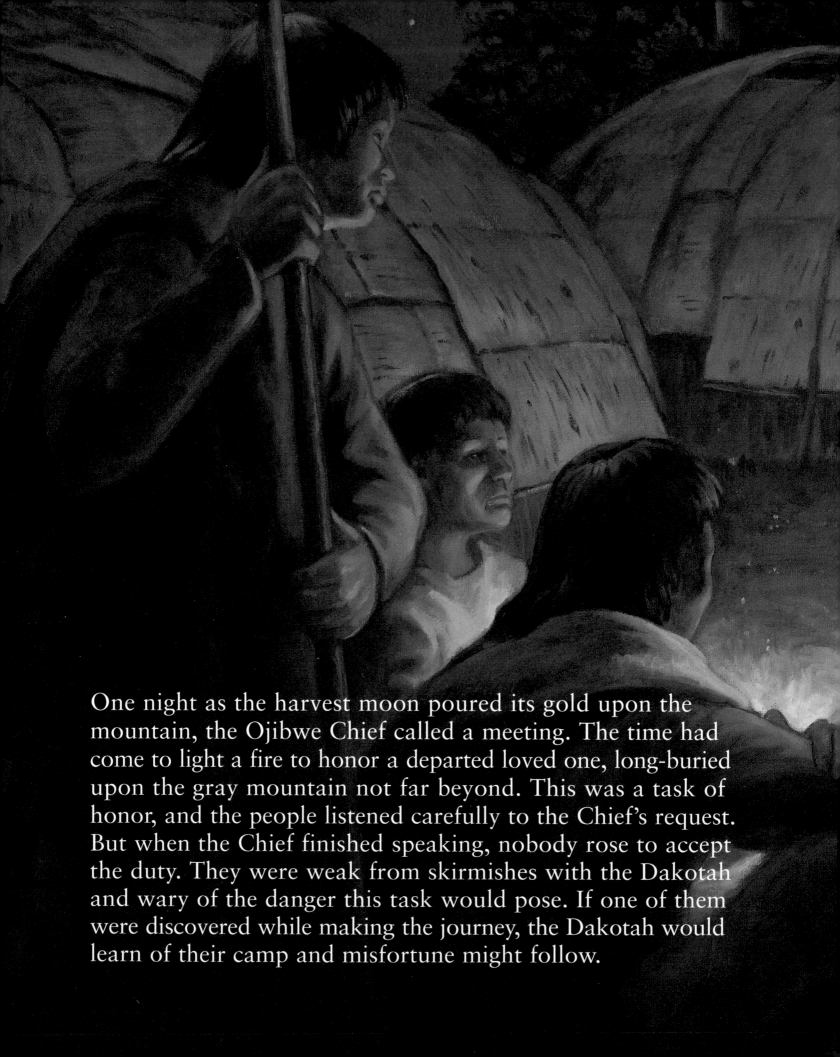

One night as the harvest moon poured its gold upon the mountain, the Ojibwe Chief called a meeting. The time had come to light a fire to honor a departed loved one, long-buried upon the gray mountain not far beyond. This was a task of honor, and the people listened carefully to the Chief's request. But when the Chief finished speaking, nobody rose to accept the duty. They were weak from skirmishes with the Dakotah and wary of the danger this task would pose. If one of them were discovered while making the journey, the Dakotah would learn of their camp and misfortune might follow.

The air was stone-cold quiet except for the snap of the fire and the rustle of embers. The silence drew heavy upon them until a young girl stepped forward through the smoke. Her name was Morning Fawn, and as she looked to the Chief she said, "I will do this." A milk-white falcon flew low above her head, skimming many times to circle above her. To all it was a sign that fate had chosen her for this dangerous task.

At dawn Morning Fawn followed a footpath into the woods. She stepped across a slow-moving stream where bald eagles made great nests in pine trees above her. She walked beside ponds where yellow-and-white water lilies rested upon the surface like night-stars that had fallen from the sky. She rested among stands of white birch and balsam poplar, and then walked until the path became a soft carpet of aged pine needles broken by knotted cedar roots that twisted their way across the forest floor.

As Morning Fawn reached the sacred place, she felt at peace with her task and prepared for her fate. She carefully lit the flame and bowed her head.

Now it was time to make the journey home.

As she made her way through the woods, she saw
a young Dakotah brave lying upon the ground.

At first, Morning Fawn stood as still and silent as a mother deer hiding her young in an open meadow. But when her eyes met his she could tell that he was very ill and did not have long to live. Pale and weak, he was warm to the touch. Morning Fawn made him a bed out of leaves and started a fire to cook some broth. He lay there quietly as she stroked his hair with a friendly touch. Although barely able to speak, he told her an old healing secret. Doing as he said, Morning Fawn gathered the root of the balsam poplar and carefully made a special medicine for him.

Morning Fawn remained with the Dakotah brave for three days and three nights. With her help, he grew stronger and was no longer pale. During this time he told her of his home where bright meadows went sweeping toward the sun, and she told him of shady granite resting spots near the edge of the red-stained lake. He sang to her about the shaggy bison and the great thunder they made during the hunt, and she motioned upward to describe the dancing skies and how bands of blue and green and pink seemed to flash in the night. They laughed often and liked each other very much. But deep inside Morning Fawn knew they would not be able to remain together. Until their bands were no longer enemies, such a friendship would not be allowed.

Back at the village, there was great worry when Morning Fawn had not returned after the sacred fire was lit. Two braves went to find her and came upon Morning Fawn with the Dakotah brave. Worried the boy might tell his tribe about the Ojibwe camp, they quickly took him prisoner.

When they reached the village, the boy was set apart from the others. He was lonely and frightened, and Morning Fawn wanted to help him.

That night when the last fire cooled and the village was sleeping,
Morning Fawn set him free. The pair slipped quietly into the
forest to a stand of balsam poplar. Then, as the dusky moon cast
shadows upon their faces, Morning Fawn told him to go away.

But the Dakotah boy did not understand.
He did not want to leave his friend. She had saved
his life, and he wanted to be with her always.

Morning Fawn did not want harm to come his way, so she
insisted he leave. Still he did not understand. He begged to stay
while she kept telling him to go away. With tears in his eyes he
asked her to live with him upon the prairie, but Morning Fawn
refused. Dawn was breaking and she was worried that he might
be discovered. At last Morning Fawn knew of only one way
to make him go home. Although she cared for him very much,
Morning Fawn told him otherwise and ordered him to leave.

When others learned that Morning Fawn had let the boy free, they would not look in her direction or speak to her. This went on for days and weeks, and Morning Fawn felt sad and alone.

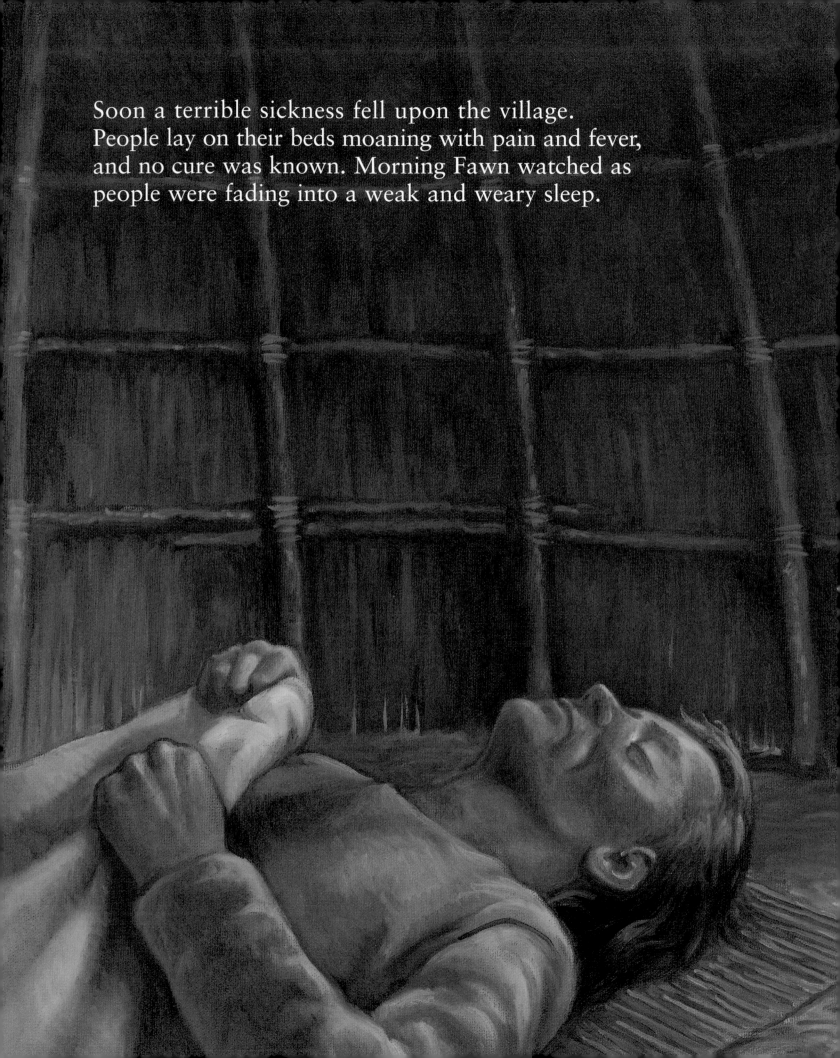

Soon a terrible sickness fell upon the village.
People lay on their beds moaning with pain and fever,
and no cure was known. Morning Fawn watched as
people were fading into a weak and weary sleep.

Then she remembered the secret the Dakotah boy had shared. Doing as he had taught her, she gathered the root of the balsam poplar and made the healing balm, and went from bed to bed. One by one, the sick began to feel better, and others who lay waiting began to call out for her. *"Mah-nu-sa-tia! Mah-nu-sa-tia!"* they called, for that was the name by which they knew the balsam poplar. For many days the sick kept calling out to her, *"Mah-nu-sa-tia! Mah-nu-sa-tia!"* and in time, she was able to heal them all. So in the spirit of their renewed love for her they renamed her "Mahnusatia" and all was forgiven.

The time came for the Ojibwe to move their camp. When they did, Mahnusatia stayed behind, remaining beneath the balsam poplar. Every evening she sang her farewell to the Dakotah boy and her words carried high upon the wind and throughout the land.

Each year as her people passed the balsam poplar they would call out to her "*Mah-nu-sa-tia! Mah-nu-sa-tia!*," as a sign of great respect.

Years passed and Mahnusatia grew old and small, withering deep into the earth itself. Since that time, generations still call out her name when they pass the balsam poplar, the name chosen to address the beautiful land that lay west of the great unsalted sea. And as it came to be spoken in new accents and languages through time, we still hear her name today, known throughout the world and in the hearts of those who will love her always.

Mahnusatia! Mahnusatia!
Minnesota! Minnesota!

Kathy-jo Wargin

Author Kathy-jo Wargin has earned national acclaim with numerous best-selling children's titles such as *The Edmund Fitzgerald: Song of the Bell*. Born in Tower, Minnesota, and inspired by the cultural stories she heard as a child, Kathy-jo has dedicated her career to exploring the folklore of the Upper Midwest. In addition to *The Legend of Minnesota*, she is also the author of the award-winning books, *The Legend of Sleeping Bear*; *The Legend of the Lady's Slipper*, an Upper Midwest Bookseller's Favorite; and *The Legend of the Loon*, an IRA Children's Choice Book. She is also the author of *V is for Viking: A Minnesota Alphabet*, a Northeastern Minnesota Book Award Winner and a Minnesota Book Award Finalist. Kathy-jo currently lives with her family in Petoskey, Michigan.

David Geister

Artist David Geister has entertained audiences for years with his costumed portrayals of historic characters from the nineteenth century, such as the painters Seth Eastman and George Catlin, as well as the 1820s inhabitants of Minnesota's Historic Fort Snelling. The illustrations for *The Legend of Minnesota* continue this rich tradition of story-telling with beautifully rendered characters and dramatic scenes of Minnesota's northern landscape.

David lives with his wife, Pat Bauer, and stepdaughters, Eva and Allison, in Minneapolis, Minnesota. Their two cats, Monet and Matisse, and wiener dog, Zoe, keep him company and occasionally offer advice while he paints. *The Legend of Minnesota* is David's first children's book.